T0365798

Bessie

Written by Mark E. Scheyder

AuthorHouse™ LLC
1663 Liberty Drive
Bloomington, IN 47403
www.authorhouse.com
Phone: 1-800-839-8640

Published by AuthorHouse 08/20/2014

ISBN: 978-1-4969-3439-0 (sc)
ISBN: 978-1-4969-3440-6 (e)

Library of Congres Control Number: 2014948578

Bessie

CHAPTER 1

Quite a few years ago, in a factory in Detroit, a tiny little truck came to be. In-between giant trucks with huge bodies and dual wheels and supercharged Mustangs and slick minivans, this little truck came off the assembly line steel gray with nothing to boast about.

Mark
BESSIE

She was built on a Wednesday, which means that the engineers in charge of her were well in stride. They made no mistakes on her. Her main engineer, a man named Mark, made sure she was perfect. He secretly called her *Bessie*, and he put his initials inside her rear bumper. To him, she was special. Her little hand crank windows worked like a charm. Her radio was delightful. Her little engine performed with splendor. They painted her a beautiful cherry red. But she was still just a little plain truck. No frills. Just a simple little Ranger girl.

The giant pickups, fancy Mustangs, and slick minivans made terrible fun of her. “She’s small,” they said. “She has no power.” They said she would never amount to anything. They thought she would break down in a week. They laughed and laughed, and the little red Ranger held her head down in shame. She had no idea why they even built her.

FACTORY

Yet, the little truck had a heart, and she had hope. She believed she was going to survive. She knew that somewhere, someday, her knight would arrive and make her a special little truck.

The little red Ranger sat in the factory storage lot for weeks. No one paid any attention to her. It was as if she were one big mistake. She couldn't understand why no one would take her and make her their own. She was bright and pretty, clean, new, and ready to drive. Yet no one came. She was like an orphan.

Then, one day, she woke up from a wonderful dream. She dreamed of a life where someone would really care for her. She dreamed of the nice man who had taken such good care of her in the factory. Then, she discovered that she was being loaded onto a huge truck with many other trucks. The other trucks picked on her and bumped into her on purpose. They laughed at her. "Where am I going?" she asked. But no one paid her one bit of attention. She hoped so much that she was finally going somewhere she would be happy. *If only I could get away from all these big bully trucks*, she thought.

The little red Ranger traveled for what seemed like forever. On and on they went. Down one highway and then another. Then, finally, they arrived at a place that wasn't very pretty. The little red Ranger's hopes began to dwindle. "Where am I going?" she asked. "Who is my owner?" But no one paid her any mind. Off the truck she came. Brutally dropped. A man with dirty boots and oily gloves jumped into her driver's seat and drove her into a warehouse. It was a little seashore town in New Jersey.

CHAPTER 2

The little red Ranger was exhausted. She was so sad. She just knew that her new life was going to be nothing but labor. She discovered that her whole reason for being was to simply be a worker truck at a company called Pack and Ship. Her dreams of traveling beautiful highways and byways next to blue seas and green forests were just that—*dreams* that would never be. She cried. Little pools of tears formed under the front of her little-engine-that-could. How could life be so unfair? All she wanted to do was belong. She wanted to bring groceries home, give the kids and the dog a ride in her pickup bed, and do anything else that a kind owner or family would ask of her. She wanted to get a bath on the weekends. She wanted to look pretty and make her family proud. But that wasn't to be.

The next morning, the little red Ranger was moved into the shop where the doctor could inspect her. He saw that she had been crying, and he discovered that, even though she was brand new, she had a fever. Well, he knew how to remedy that, and he did so in short order. He wiped her eyes, cleared her throat, and gave her a good dose of coolant. He declared the little red Ranger ready for duty. And duty it was.

PACK N' SHIP

CHAPTER 3

The little red Ranger went to work on a Monday morning when she was barely a year old. She had only ever been driven eight miles. By that evening, she had 220 miles on her odometer. They loaded package after package into her cargo bed, and she carried them dutifully. By the end of the week, she had driven two thousand miles. Every night when she came into the warehouse, she was exhausted. But the doctor would come out and keep her well. He made sure her little engine was working in top condition. He would replace parts, oil, and the little red Ranger's lifeblood. Her heart continued to beat and she would occasionally feel a surge of pride. She never broke down. She was doing the job she was meant to do. She was a worker truck.

Yet, she was sad. The big trucks still made fun of her. They would laugh and pull up next to her and *varoom* their engines. The little red Ranger would jump in a panic. No one loved her or really cared about her. But she still dreamed of a day when someone kind would come and not smoke cigarettes in her. Someone who wouldn't slam her door at the end of the day. Someone who would say thanks for a job well done. It just didn't seem like it was ever going to happen!

TOWING

The little red Ranger worked and worked for seven long years. Day in and day out. She delivered over a million packages throughout that seashore town. Finally, the owners of the delivery company decided that the little red Ranger was finished, worn out, and used up. She had driven 120 thousand miles. They felt it was time to put her out to pasture, so they retired her. She didn't even remember leaving Pack and Ship. A big tow truck came, and they loaded her tired little body onboard. The big truck could tell that the little red Ranger was no quitter. Quietly, he told her never ever to give up. He said, "Little red Ranger, I can see that you have worked so very hard, and I know that soon life for you is going to be better. I just know that someone nice is going to find you and make you part of their family." And Bessie once again had hope.

BESSIE

CHAPTER 4

Bessie awoke one pretty morning near the sleepy town of Cape May. She didn't know why she all of a sudden thought of herself as *Bessie*. It just came to her. Maybe it was a memory from something she had heard a long time ago. She'd been *the red Ranger* for so long at Pack and Ship that she just decided to give herself a name. It didn't matter if no one knew it. She was tired of not having a real name. She was somebody, and she liked the name Bessie.

FOR SALE

That morning, a man in overalls was washing and waxing her. She wasn't in the ugly, depressing warehouse anymore. She was in a pretty yard with trees and flowers. There were pretty birds and butterflies. One butterfly even landed on her mirror. It felt really nice to get scrubbed down. Her wheels were clean, her windows were bright, and her eyes were clear. It was like getting a nice back scratch. *What was happening? Was there a new life in store? Would anybody want a little red Ranger that had been used so harshly?* she wondered. And she waited. The man in the overalls moved her to a shady spot under a pretty oak tree. Little birds landed on her and sang to her. Bessie rested her tired and worn body, and then the man put a *for sale* sign on her. This wasn't to be Bessie's new home.

AUTO FIND
SEARCH RESULTS: 0
AUTO
CLASSIFIEDS
CAR FIND
AUTO ADS
TRUCKS
ZERO RESULT
CLASSIFIEDS CARS

CHAPTER 5

Not far away, in the little seashore town of Ocean City, lived a man. He had moved there from Detroit. He was fairly wealthy. He had made his fortune designing and building little trucks. He had a beautiful home and two beautiful daughters. Yet he was tired of fancy cars and all the trappings that go with being rich. His daughters had grown up, married, and moved away. He longed for the feeling of the open road in one of his trucks. He was lonely, too. He searched the newspaper advertisements, the Internet, and everywhere for the perfect little truck. He thought about his days in Detroit when he had built his very first truck—the one he named Bessie. He remembered how beautiful she was in her simplicity. She didn't have all the bells and whistles of the luxury cars and trucks of today. Oh, but she had been sound, solid, and he had built her to last. Yet his search came up empty. There was no good little truck to be found.

FOR SALE

CHAPTER 6

It was a pretty morning in that sleepy town outside of Cape May. As the man from Detroit was driving down the road, he saw a pretty little red Ranger in a nice yard with a *for sale* sign. The truck was bright, polished, and shiny. He just had to stop to inquire. He wasn't sure, and he really couldn't believe his eyes, but what he saw just about stopped his heart. He got out of his car and touched the little red Ranger's hood. He looked at its little engine and inside her cab. Then he looked at the inside of the back bumper and saw the tiny initials he had put there so many years before. So many memories came flooding back. He remembered the tiny little truck he had been instructed to build. He remembered her simplicity. He remembered how hard he had worked to make her strong and safe, even though she wasn't a muscle car. He remembered how proud he had been when she came off the line, ready to roll. He stood there and said, "Bessie, is that *you?*"

CHAPTER 7

Bessie woke up in an instant. It was as if she heard a voice from a very long time ago. *Maybe I'm still dreaming*, she thought. After all, the birds and butterflies were still singing and tickling her. But she *knew* that voice. She had heard it so very long ago, and it was a pleasant, kind, and gentle voice. She wanted to hear more. So, with great effort, she wiped the sleep from her eyes, pumped up her tired springs, and stood tall to see who was paying attention to her. In an instant, she recognized the man. It was *him*, the man who had built her! How could he have possibly found her after all these years in a place so far away from where she had started life? But there he was, talking to the man in the coveralls.

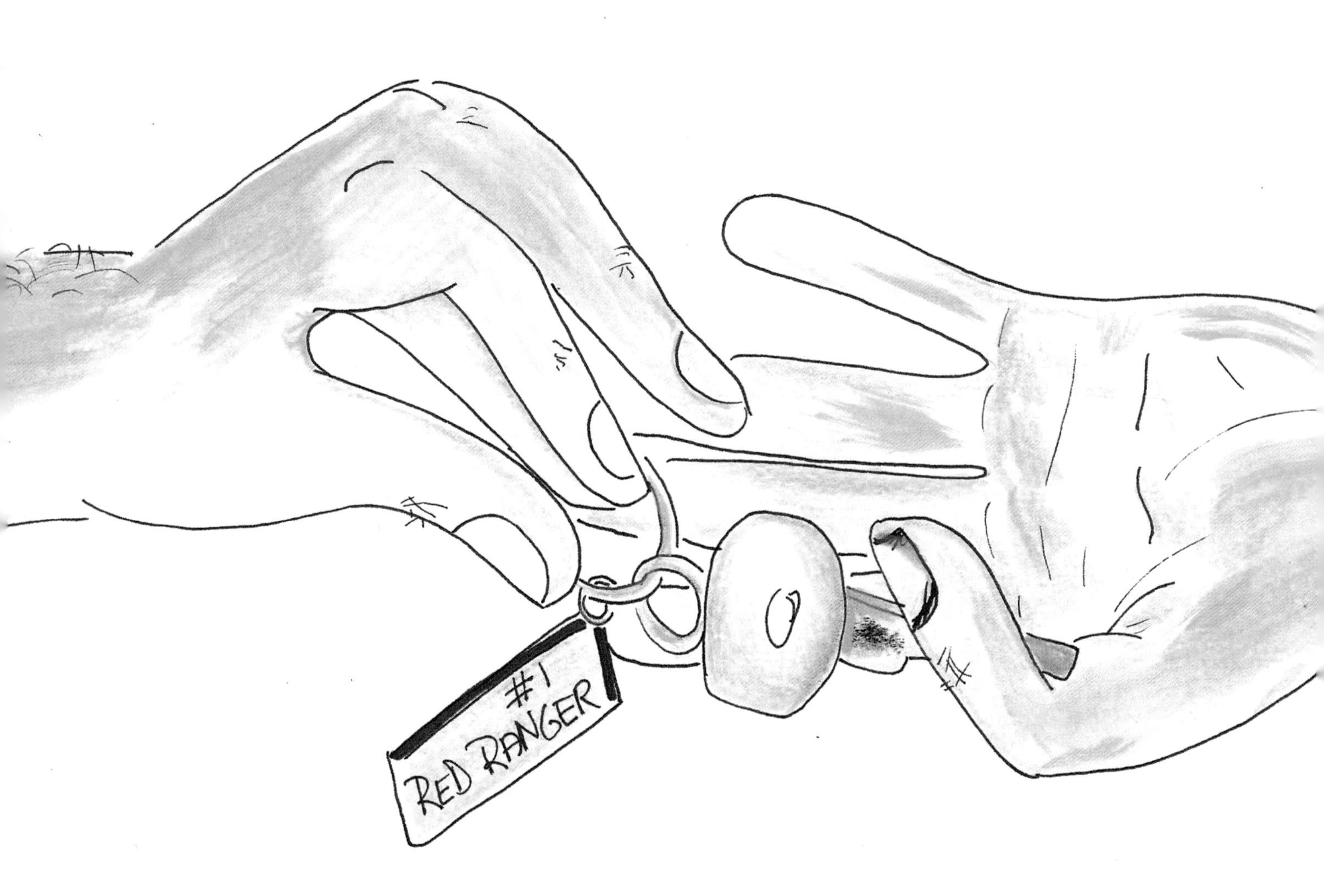
#1
RED RANGER

It didn’t take long. Bessie saw the man hand some money to the man in the coveralls. The man in the coveralls gave the man from Detroit the keys to little Bessie’s heart. And Bessie smiled. She had come home.

Bessie
&
MARK

The man from Detroit, Mark, came back over to Bessie. “Hold on, little girl,” he said. “You’re coming home with me tomorrow.” Bessie just smiled and smiled. No tears. She was going home! A little cardinal landed on her roof and said, “Isn’t it wonderful, Bessie? You’ve finally got a real home after all these years.” And Bessie pumped up her chest with pride and joy. Was it possible? Could fate finally be changing? Could the used up little red Ranger finally belong somewhere special? For the first time in her little truck life, little Bessie believed that happiness might just be possible. And it was all because of one man who cared.

CHAPTER 8

The very next day, Mark came and picked up Bessie. He knew she needed help. She was all pretty on the outside but she shuddered and swerved. She didn't steer well either. Her little engine coughed and couldn't breathe well. So Mark took Bessie straight to the doctor. Well, the good doctor performed miracles.

He made Bessie well again. He gave her new springs. He fixed her little engine so that it ran like new. And Bessie once again drove straight and true without coughing. She was proud. She didn't care what any of the old big trucks with the big tires had to say. As a matter of fact, she even passed one on the road. It was one of the trucks that had made fun of her at that factory in Detroit. It was limping along and very old and worn out.

There was Bessie, standing tall for the little red Ranger that she was. She was excited about her new life and the new adventures that awaited her.

Alaska
FloRidA

Bessie made many trips throughout the great country of America. She drove to Alaska, then from Alaska to Florida, and then from Florida up the east coast back to South Jersey where she met more family and friends. She had seen the beautiful blue waters of the Pacific, the rough and turbulent Atlantic Ocean, and the amazing tall Douglas firs of the Northwest. She has seen Denali, the "Great One" in Alaska, and she had camped gleefully under her shadow in a pristine valley at Wonder Lake. She even let a little black bear climb into her pickup bed and take a nap. She came head-to-head with a beautiful mama moose. They smiled at each other, and the little baby moose kissed her. Bessie was the happiest little red Ranger in the whole wide world. Everyone wanted to be with her.

Today, little Bessie lives in south Florida in a little town called Naples. She's very happy there. She has a beautiful home and a quiet garage for her bedroom. The man from Detroit wakes her up every morning, and they take a nice little drive just to see the beauty of the world. They drive past the Gulf of Mexico and wave at the dolphins. The dolphins sing back and say, "Hi, Bessie. You look wonderful!"

7555

Bessie backs into her driveway and there sits a tiny little bunny rabbit. The bunny rabbit and Bessie are good friends. Bessie stops short so Bunny can jump out of the way. Somehow, even though you can't hear them, you know they are talking. Bunny runs to the front to look at Bessie and asks her how her drive was. Bessie looks down at Bunny and simply smiles. *My drive with Mark was wonderful. We saw the ocean, dolphins jumping, the cypress forest, and the busy streets of the city. We saw the Everglades and alligators. We stopped and rescued a big tortoise and put him back in the lake. Now we're back home and I get to hang out with you, my furry bunny friend.*

Happy

Nowadays, Bessie the little red Ranger has the biggest smile on her little red truck face! She is home, she is cared for, and she is happy! She brings home groceries and gives the family dog a ride in her bed.

Happy!

The End

ABOUT THE AUTHOR

Mark E. Scheyder lives in Naples, Florida. He has a diverse career working for the FAA in System Engineering. He recently started writing children's books, which have been a passion for many years. *Bessie* is the first in a series.

Illustrator Amber Watkins was born and raised in southern New Jersey. Amber attended Regent University and earned a BS in Business. She began sketching at a young age and found her love of watercolors and acrylics. Since then, she has enjoyed using mixed media to bring her sketches to life.

ABOUT THIS BOOK

The story about Bessie will encourage both young and old to never give up hope, even though life has its ups and downs. Directed at a young audience, it is essential that children persevere and overcome adversity. Even if bullies push one around, one still has skills, talents, and people who care. Never lose heart.

Printed in the United States
By Bookmasters